What's that Noise?

Sally Prue
Illustrated by Desideria Guicciardini

RIGBY

Ryan liked playing with his trains.

"Look at all these trains!" cried Dad.

"I'll clear them away," said Ryan.

"Then it's bedtime," said Mum.

That night, Ryan had a dream. He dreamed
that some men were digging a hole.
The hole was so big that a giant white rabbit
hopped out of it.
The rabbit had big feet that banged on
the ground. Bang! Bang! BANG!

Ryan woke up.

The giant white rabbit had gone.

But something was still going bang!

Bang! BANG!

"Mum!" shouted Ryan.

The banging stopped.

"Mum, what was all that banging?"
asked Ryan.
"It's nothing," said Mum. "Go back to sleep."
"But 'nothing' is quiet," thought Ryan.

The next day, everything was quiet.
Ryan came home from school and played with
his trains.
Then he had tea.

"What was all that banging last night?"
he asked Dad.
"I don't know," said Dad. "Maybe it was the
water pipes. They make banging noises
sometimes."

That night, Ryan heard the banging again.
He was glad it was just the water pipes.

Bang! Bang! Bang! went the water pipes.

Bang! Bang! OUCH!

"What was that?" thought Ryan.

The next day, everything was quiet.
Ryan came home from school and played with
his trains.
Then he had tea.

"That banging came back last night," said
Ryan. "It went 'ouch'!"
"Well, it could have been a cat," said Dad,
"with a bad foot."

That night, the banging was worse than ever!
BANG! BANG! BANG!

Ryan couldn't sleep. Something terrible must be
going on.

Something so bad that no one would tell him
what it was.

The next day, everything was quiet.
Ryan came home from school, but he was too
tired to play with his trains.

"I want to sleep down here tonight," said Ryan. "Away from all the banging."
"It's all right," said Dad. "The banging won't come back. And I have something to show you. Come with me."

Ryan and Dad went up the ladder to the loft.

"A train layout!" said Ryan. "You've made me a train layout!"

Ryan was so happy he jumped up and down. Bang! Bang! BANG! went his feet on the hard floor.

And he didn't mind a bit.

BANG!
BANG!
BANG!